Thank You, Ruth & Naomi

Written by **Charlotte Lundy**
Illustrated by **Miriam Sagasti**

THANK YOU, RUTH & NAOMI

Text Copyright © 2004 by Charlotte Lundy
Illustrations Copyright © 2003 by Miriam Sagasti

The illustrations in this book were rendered in watercolor.

FIRST PRINTING

Published by Bay Light Publishing, Inc.
        Mooresville, North Carolina

Layout and Production by Heather Claremont Sullivan
        6925 Brandon Chase Lane, Concord, NC 28025

Printed in Korea

Publisher's Cataloging-in-Publication
(Provided by Quality Books, Inc.)

Lundy, Charlotte.
    Thank You, Ruth & Naomi / written by Charlotte Lundy ;
illustrated by Miriam Sagasti. --1 st ed.
    p. cm.
    Includes bibliographical references.
    SUMMARY: The Biblical story of Ruth and Naomi teaches
Keana about the true meaning of friendship.
    Audience: Ages 3-10.
    ISBN 0-9741817 -0-6
    LCCN 2003094501

    1. Friendship--Juvenile fiction. 2. Ruth (Biblical
figure)--Juvenile fiction. 3. Naomi (Biblical
character)--Juvenile fiction. 4. Bible stories, English
--O.T.--Ruth. [1. Friendship--Fiction. 2. Ruth
(Biblical figure)--Fiction. 3. Naomi (Biblical
character)--Fiction. 4. Bible stories--O.T.]
I. Sagasti, Miriam. II. Title.

PZ7.L97887Tm 2004   [E]
                            QBI33-1500

Dear Jesus,

Thank you for coming into my heart and being my best friend.

Help me to show your love to other people so you can be their best friend, too.

I love you, Jesus.
Your friend,
Charlie

~ A Child's Prayer ~

This book is dedicated to
Marsha, Evelyn and Carolyn,
who are not only my sisters but my best friends as well.

Keana and her mother are on their way to Ashley's house. They are going to a movie tonight and then spending the night at Keana's house.

Keana is really looking forward to this day. Ashley is her very best friend. They have been best friends since the first grade! Now they are in the third grade. Every weekend they play together at each other's house.

At the movies, they went to see
"The Lady and The Tramp."
They both liked the part where
the two dogs were eating a
piece of spaghetti and
accidentally met in the middle!

After the movies, they went to
Keana's house and played
some games. It was so much
fun having her best friend over
to play!

The next day was Sunday. Keana and Ashley both go to the same church and are in the same Sunday School class. Today, there was a new girl in their class. Her name was Grace. Ashley had already met Grace because she had moved in across the street from her. She thought Grace was very nice.

Monday at school, Keana overheard Ashley invite Grace over to play. Keana was so sad when she heard this. How could her very best friend hurt her feelings like this? All of the way home from school, Keana was so quiet. She was sad that Ashley had found a new best friend.

That night at the dinner table, Keana's mother noticed how sad she looked. While they were cleaning up the kitchen, Keana's mother asked her why she was being so quiet.

Keana said, "Mom, you're not going to believe this, but Ashley has found a new best friend.

"What makes you think that?" asked Keana's mother.

"Well, today at school I heard Ashley invite Grace over to play at her house. I guess that they are going to be best friends now," said Keana.

Keana's mother gave her a big hug and said,
"Just because Ashley invited Grace over for one day to
play doesn't mean that they are going to be best friends.
Good friends like you and Ashley last a lifetime.
But even though you two are best friends doesn't mean
that both of you can't have other friends also. Let me
tell you a story about two best friends in the Bible
named Ruth and Naomi."

This was the story Keana's mother told her:

"A long time ago in the Bible, there was a lady named Naomi. She was married to a man named Elimelech. They had two sons. Their two sons got married and their wives were named Ruth and Orpah. They all lived in a town called Moab.

Before long, Naomi's husband died and she was left with her two sons and their wives. After about ten years, Naomi's two sons died. Then Naomi was left with just her two daughters-in-law.

A short time after that, Naomi told Ruth and Orpah to go back home to their people. She wanted them to find new husbands. Naomi said, "May the Lord show kindness to you as you have shown to your dead and me."

Orpah kissed her mother-in-law and said, "Goodbye," but Ruth would not leave Naomi. Ruth said to Naomi, "Do not tell me to leave you. Where you go, I will go. Where you stay, I will stay. Your people will be my people. Where you die, I will die and be buried there."

So Ruth and Naomi returned to Bethlehem. It was there that Ruth found a husband to love and take care of her and Naomi. Ruth was working in the fields one day when she was noticed by a man named Boaz.

Not too long after that, Boaz married Ruth
and took her and Naomi into his home.

Ruth and Boaz had a son named Obed. Naomi
was so proud of Ruth and her new grandson.
Throughout all of their years together, Ruth and
Naomi remained good friends in spite of everything
that happened to them. This is what true friendship
is all about."

"Wow!" said Keana, "That was a great story."

When Keana saw Ashley the next day at school, they waved to each other and had lunch together. Ashley asked Keana if she was coming over this weekend. Keana was so happy. She said, "You want me to come over this weekend?"

"Well, sure I do!" said Ashley.
"We're best friends aren't we?"

Keana smiled and said, "Yes, we are!"

When Keana got home from school that day,
she hugged her mother, looked up to the sky and said, "Thank You, God,
for sending Ruth and Naomi to show me what true friendship is all about."

The End